For Barbara, Dave and Emily

Also by Hilda Offen in Happy Cat Books

Elephant Pie
Good Girl, Gracie Growler!
Umbrella Weather

HAPPY CAT BOOKS

Published by Happy Cat Books Ltd.,
Bradfield, Essex CO11 2UT, UK

This edition first published 2004
Copyright © Hilda Offen 1992

A CIP catalogue record for this book is available from the British Library

ISBN 1 903285 69 0

Printed in China by Midas Printing International Ltd.

Nice Work, Little Wolf!

Hilda Offen

Happy Cat Books

Mrs Wolf and Little Wolf lived in a tumbledown house.

There were holes in the roof and holes in the walls.

One day Little Wolf fell through a rotten floorboard.

'I can't stand this a moment longer!' said Mrs Wolf.

'I shall go to the builder's yard and buy a hammer and nails.'

She popped Little Wolf in his pram and set off for town.

On her way Mrs Wolf met a friend and they stopped to talk.

'This is really boring,' said Little Wolf to himself.

'I'm going to have some fun.'

He climbed out of his pram and was over a fence

in the twinkling of an eye.

He rolled down a bank and landed at the bottom with a *crash!*

'Go and see what has landed in our cucumber frame,
my dearest!' said Mr Porker to his wife.

'Look in the cucumber frame, dear!' said Mrs Porker
to her daughter Brenda.

'Look in the frame!' said Brenda to her brother Brian.

Brian Porker had no one to order about, so he went into the garden. He came back holding Little Wolf by the tail.

'It's a cat!' said Mr Porker.

'It's a ferret!' said Mrs Porker.

'It's a rat!' said Brenda.

'It's a tiny dog!' said Brian. 'I shall teach it to do tricks!'

They went out on to the lawn.

'Jump through this hoop!' said Brian.

'There's no dinner if you don't!'

He made Little Wolf sit up and beg and taught him

to balance a football on his nose.

'Do go and fetch the Sunday papers, my love!'

said Mr Porker the next morning.

'Go and fetch the papers, dear!' said Mrs Porker to Brenda.

'Fetch the papers!' said Brenda to Brian.

'Fetch!' said Brian to Little Wolf.

Little Wolf ran all the way to the paper shop.

Then he ran all the way back, carrying the papers in his mouth.

The Porkers snatched them and lazed around till lunch-time.

'This house is in a shocking state!'
said Mr Porker.

'Clean it up, will you, my sweet?'

'Clean up the house, dear!'
said Mrs Porker to Brenda.

'Clean the house!'
said Brenda to Brian.

'Clean it!'
said Brian to Little Wolf.

So Little Wolf dusted and hoovered
and did the washing-up.
The Porkers went upstairs
and had a nap.

Little Wolf began to grow. Soon his jump suit wouldn't stretch any more, so he had to wear one of Brian's sailor suits instead.

'The fence needs painting!' said Mr Porker.
'Will you see to it, honey-pie?'
'Go and paint the fence, dear!' said Mrs Porker to Brenda.

'Paint the fence!' said Brenda to Brian.

'Paint it!' said Brian to Little Wolf.

So Little Wolf took a brush and a pot of paint and painted the fence
a beautiful shade of blue.

The Porkers sat under the trees and watched.

Before long, Little Wolf grew out of Brian's sailor suit. He had to wear one of Brenda's frocks.

'The garden looks like a jungle!'
said Mr Porker.
'Tidy it up, won't you,
my little blossom?'
'Tidy up the garden, dear!'
said Mrs Porker to Brenda.
'Tidy up the garden!'
said Brenda to Brian.
'Tidy it up!'
said Brian to Little Wolf.

So Little Wolf mowed the lawn
and dug the flower-beds
and planted new trees.
The Porkers strolled about
and sniffed the roses.

Little Wolf was growing sideways as well as up.
Soon Brenda's frock was too short and tight and he had to wear
one of Mrs Porker's old ball gowns.

The weather got hotter and hotter.
'Please go outside and dig a swimming-pool, my pet!'
said Mr Porker.

'Go and dig a swimming-pool, dear!' said Mrs Porker to Brenda.

'Dig a pool!' said Brenda to Brian.

'Dig!' said Brian to Little Wolf.

So Little Wolf took a spade and dug a deep hole in the garden.

Then he tiled it and filled it with water.

The Porkers put on their swimming costumes and jumped in.

Soon Little Wolf was too big for Mrs Porker's ball-gown.

He had to wear one of Mr Porker's boiler suits.

One day Brian made Little Wolf show the Porkers a new trick.

'The dog is getting very big!' said Mr Porker.

We need a larger house. Could you build one, my poppet?'

'Build a new house, dear!' said Mrs Porker to Brenda.

'Build a house!' said Brenda to Brian.

'Start building!' said Brian to Little Wolf.

So Little Wolf went to the builder's
yard and bought bricks and tiles
and timber. He built the Porkers
a fine new house.
He hammered so hard that
the buttons popped off
his boiler suit.

Then Little Wolf cooked bean stew for the Porkers in their
new kitchen. Mr Porker dropped his spoon on the floor.
'Pick up my spoon, will you, sweetheart?' said Mr Porker.
'Pick up your father's spoon, dear!' said Mrs Porker to Brenda.

'Pick up Dad's spoon!' said Brenda to Brian.

'Pick it up!' said Brian to Little Wolf.

And at last Little Wolf lost his temper. He took a deep breath.

'No!' he roared. 'I won't!'

He was so angry that he burst right out of his boiler suit.

'Help!' cried the Porkers as Little Wolf chased them
down the garden path.

When he reached the gate Little Wolf stopped.

He threw back his head and howled.

'Mum!' howled Little Wolf. **'I want my Mum!'**

Miles away, in her tumbledown house, Mrs Wolf pricked up her ears.

She ran all the way to the Porkers' front gate.

'My baby!' she cried. 'How you've grown!'

The Porkers had gone for good, so Little Wolf asked

his mother to come in.

'What a lovely place!' said Mrs Wolf and she admired the house

and the garden and the swimming-pool.

'It's all my own work!' said Little Wolf.

Then they sat down together in their new home

and finished up the bean stew.